A Christmas Wish

For Joseph and William
—Marcus

CIP Data is available.

Published in the United States 2003 by Dutton Children's Books,
a division of Penguin Young Readers Group
345 Hudson Street, New York, New York 10014
www.penguinputnam.com

Originally published in Great Britain 2003 as *A Winter's Tale* by Templar Publishing,
an imprint of The Templar Company plc, Surrey
Designed by Mike Jolley
Manufactured in Hong Kong

First American Edition

1 3 5 7 9 10 8 6 4 2

ISBN 0-525-47195-2

The illustrations for this book were painted in acrylics on paper.
This book was typeset in Coronet.

by

Marcus Sedgwick

A Christmas Wish

illustrated by

Simon Bartram

Dutton Children's Books

New York

It's winter,

but it's warm . . .

and there's
no sign of snow.
I wish . . .

I wish

it would snow like it does

in my snow globe.

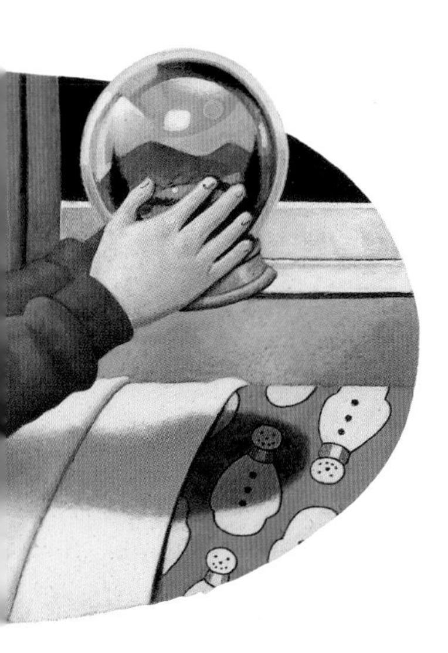

But wait!

Something

magical

is happening.

It's starting to snow!

It's starting to snow!

Just a little at first . . .

Just a little at first . . .

. . . then more and more.

This is no ordinary snowstorm!

Something
really ***magical***
is happening.

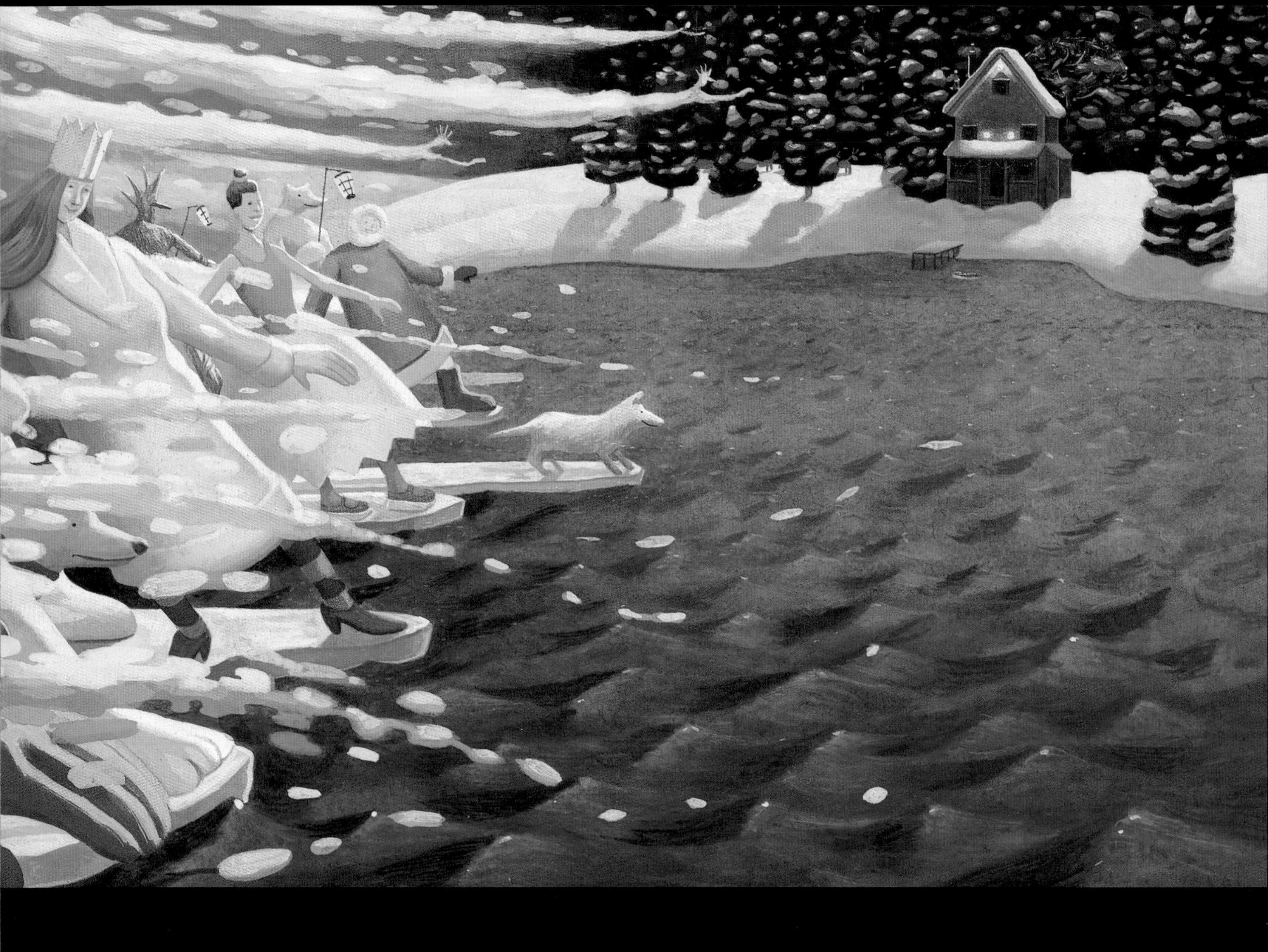

A Christmas wish
has come to life!

Morning arrives . . .

. . . and with morning,

everything

changes.

The dancing stops,

The dancing stops.

the snow subsides. . .

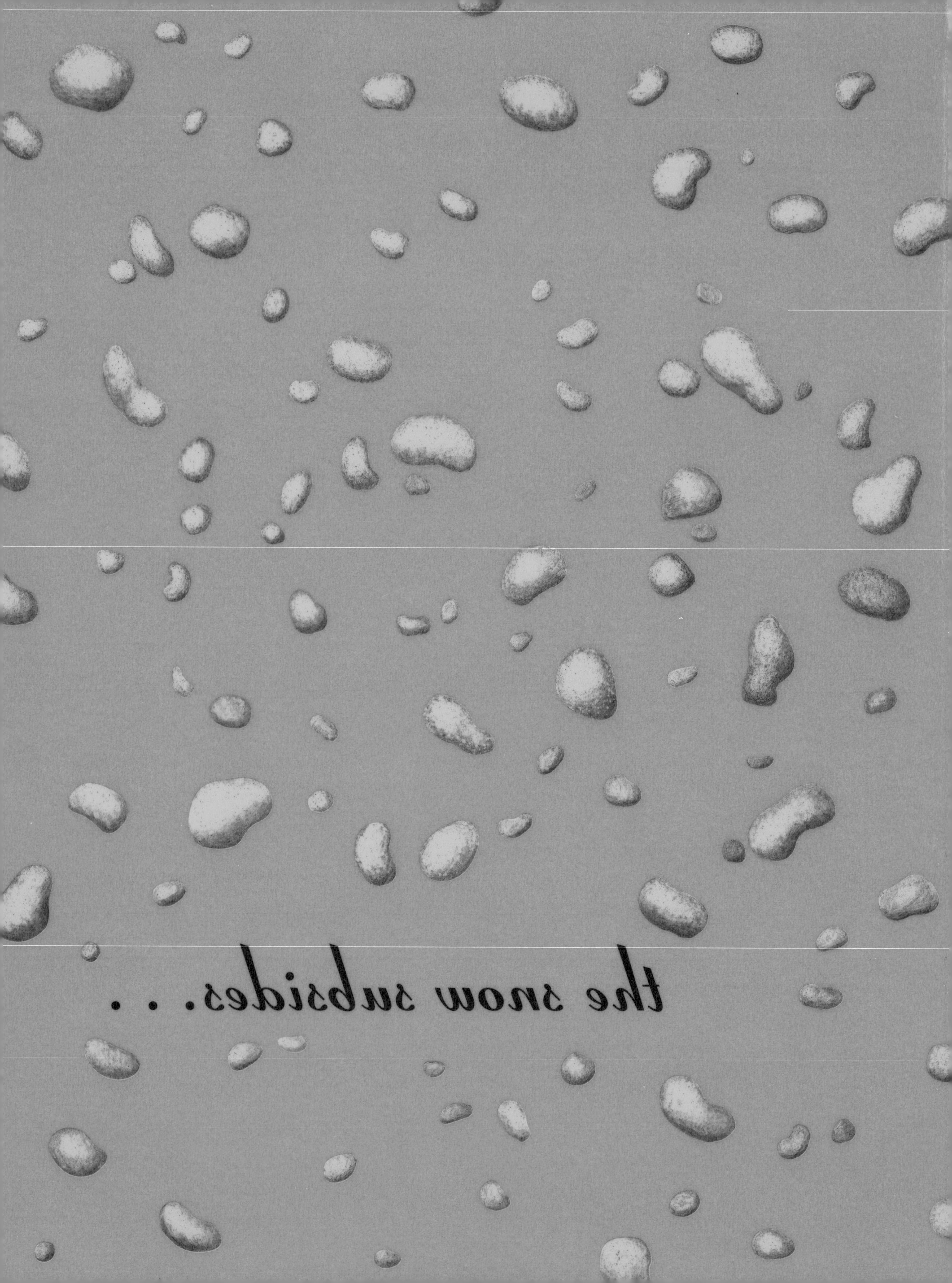
the snow subsides. . .

The magic has just begun!